Being Ben

Jacqueline Roy

illustrated by
Margaret chamberlain

WALKER
BOOKS

First published in Great Britain 2013 by Walker Books Ltd
87 Vauxhall Walk, London SE11 5HJ

2 4 6 8 10 9 7 5 3 1

Text © 2013 by Jacqueline Roy
Illustrations © 2013 Margaret Chamberlain

The right of Jacqueline Roy and Margaret Chamberlain to be identified as author and illustrator respectively of this work has been asserted by them in accordance with the Copyright, Designs and Patents Act 1988

This book has been typeset in Stempel Schneidler

Printed and bound in Great Britain by Clays Ltd, St Ives plc

British Library Cataloguing in Publication Data:
a catalogue record for this book is
available from the British Library

ISBN 978-1-4063-3306-0

www.walker.co.uk

For Tom, Dan, Emmie and Ben,
with love
J.R.

For my long-suffering
husband, Ian
M.C.

The New Baby

Ben was sitting at the kitchen table
practising his reading and stroking his dog
Wilf at the same time. His mother
was beside him, helping him
out with the words he
didn't understand.

There weren't many of these; his teacher said he was well above average at reading for someone who wasn't even eight. The story was about a boy who had a new baby brother and didn't like him much. Ben told his mother how much he sympathised. "Babies are so disgusting," he said.

His mother gave him a very odd look and said, "You don't really think that, do you? It's just that there's something we've been meaning to tell you."

Dad had been stirring the baked beans they were having for tea. The jacket potatoes were due to come out of the oven. But he stopped what he was doing and looked at Ben too, in a hopeful but worried kind of way.

This is not good, thought Ben.

His mother went on, "Soon you'll be getting a new baby brother or sister."

Ben stared at his parents as if he couldn't

believe it. He had just read the word "tragic" in his story. It meant that something was very bad. *Tragic, tragic, tragic* he thought. He buried his head in Wilf's fur. It was soft and comforting.

"Ben," said his dad, "I can't see your face. Let go of Wilf for a minute so we can talk to you."

"I don't want to." Ben's voice was muffled by Wilf's fur coat.

He thought he would be told off for being rude but his dad just said, "It's exciting, getting a brother or sister. You'll have someone to play with."

Ben was happy just as he was and he didn't want a baby brother or sister.

When he wanted to play, he could play with Mum and Dad or Wilf, or his best friends Maxine and Ollie, the twins who lived down the road. "I don't like babies," he said.

"Of course you do, Ben," his mother said.

"I don't," Ben argued. "They're horrible." And then he ran upstairs to his room and hid under his duvet.

Lying there, he thought of all the babies he knew. Fat babies, thin babies, small babies, big babies. The truth was, they were all as bad as each other and Ben was terrified of them.

They made this terrible roaring noise, day and night. It was so loud it seemed

like your ears would burst. And they were
smelly with their horrible big poos, and
their nappies needed changing all the time.
And when there was a baby in the house,
everybody thought it was wonderful and
they didn't notice anybody else, just the
squally baby.

Ben's mother came upstairs
and eased him out of the
duvet. She gave him
a hug.

"Will the
new baby
look like
me?" he
wondered.
His skin
was golden
brown and
he had curly
Afro hair.

"It might," said Mum. "Or it might be as brown as your dad or as white as me. We'll have to wait and see."

"How long do babies take to grow up?" Ben wondered.

"They can walk and talk by the time they are about two," his mother answered.

Two whole years. He didn't even want to think about it.

Maxine and Ollie came round after tea to play basketball. The three of them played in the garden, using the net that was fastened to the wall of the shed. Maxine scored the most goals, which was very annoying. She was slightly taller than the boys and she was good at blocking their shots. They sat down on the step for a while, feeling too hot and out of breath.

"My mum said we're getting a new baby," Ben announced.

Maxine touched his shirt. She hadn't
caught what he had said because his head
had been turned away from her when he'd
spoken. Although Maxine had some hearing
and she could talk a bit and lip read, she
usually did signing, as she was so much
quicker at speaking that way. The twins had
been teaching Ben sign language. He wasn't
very good at it yet but he repeated his
announcement using his hands and Maxine
signed back, "Are you happy?"

Ben couldn't answer this by signing – it was too complicated. Luckily, Maxine was a very good lip reader, so once Ben had finished explaining how fed up he was about it, she signed, "Maybe it won't be as bad as you think."

"It will be worse," growled Ben.

Ollie and Maxine smiled at each other. They were used to Ben's tendency to see the downside and found it funny at times.

They went back to playing the game. Ben was determined to beat Maxine just this once. They got noisier and noisier but no one came out to tell them to be quieter.

One of the good things about Maxine being around was that Ben could shout a lot and not get told off by Mum and Dad. She didn't need him to shout, but the adults didn't know this so they let the children make as much noise as they liked.

"I wish I had a lolly." Ollie stopped again and wiped the sweat from his freckled face.

"Me too," said Ben, "but Mum hasn't got any. We won't get anything nice for two years now."

"*Two years?*" repeated Maxine, shaking a pebble out of her sandal.

"Babies cost a lot of money to keep," replied Ben. "I wanted a new bike for my birthday. I'll never get one now." His bike was way too small. When he rode it, he had to crouch with his knees almost up to his chin. This was all right for a short time but after a while it got tiring. And he felt silly too.

"I wouldn't mind a sister," signed Maxine. Ben liked watching her sign. It looked as if she was dancing with her hands.

"You wouldn't really like another baby," said Ben gloomily. "Remember what Thomas was like when he was born."

The three of them remembered Thomas. He was Ollie and Maxine's little brother, who was now four. He had been a particularly

angry baby, not at all
sweet and soft.

"Do you remember
the nappies?" Ollie
asked Maxine.

She did. She
grinned, holding her nose.

"He broke my doll's house," Maxine
signed. She wasn't really interested in dolls,
but that didn't mean she couldn't have
a moan about the loss of her old house.
"He sat on it," she continued. "He was just
learning to stand
up and he wobbled
and fell over, crash,
right on to the side
of it. It didn't hurt
him much but
the house was
smashed to
pieces."

"Babies change things," Ben stated gloomily.

"But Thomas is OK now. He's quite good, really," said Ollie.

Ben didn't think Thomas was good at all. He was a chubby boy with huge legs that he kicked people with when they wouldn't give him a lick of their ice cream. Ben certainly didn't want a Thomas in his family.

Wilf ran into the garden to join them and Ben stroked his back. Why couldn't they just get another dog?

Then there wouldn't be any need for another brother or sister at all.

When he went to bed that night, Ben dreamt about the new baby. It was massive, with dark green hair and yellow eyes.

With one kick, it launched him almost as far as the moon. But when he described this to his mum and dad, they wouldn't believe him. They thought the new baby was the best thing ever.

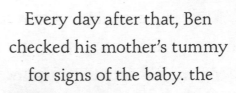

Every day after that, Ben checked his mother's tummy for signs of the baby. the bump was getting bigger and bigger, like it was going to burst at any moment. Like it was stuffed full of marshmallows. Ben knew they weren't nice, fluffy pink marshmallows. They were big, green gungey, evil marshmallows that tasted like bogies and were covered in slime. Soon the baby would come and then Ben wouldn't get a look-in any more. He would have to share his room. All his toys would get broken. And no one would even look at him – it would be baby this, and baby that, all the time.

When Ben came home from school one afternoon, his mother said, "We're going shopping. We need to buy some things so we're ready when the baby comes."

Ben hated shopping. The stores were always too hot and you had to stand around queuing for ages and ages. It was boring. He added shopping to the list of bad things that the baby was bringing into his life. And it wasn't even born yet.

The shops were packed. Ben's mum found little stretchy things called Babygros for the baby to wear when it arrived. There were stripey blue ones and stripey pink ones. Ben's mum didn't want either colour, she wanted yellow.

"I like the blue better," said Ben.

"You buy blue for a boy and pink for a girl. I don't know what the baby will be yet, so yellow would be best."

"That's silly," returned Ben. "Boys and girls should be able to wear the same."

"You're right," Mum said. "It doesn't really matter, does it?"

"Buy the blue," Ben replied. "It's definitely going to be a boy."

"How do you know?" asked his mother, smiling.

"I just do," said Ben.

They bought some of the blue ones and went to look for a buggy. Ben wanted the orange one with the teddy bears on it, even though he knew he would be jealous when he saw the

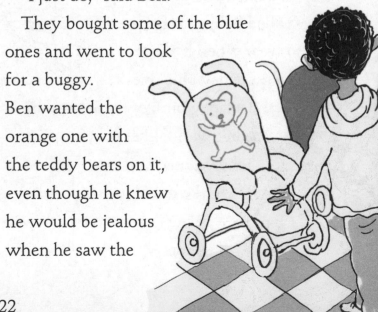

baby sitting in it. *Teddies are babyish, of
course,* he thought quickly to himself, but he
still liked them. It didn't seem fair though
that the new baby was getting so much
nice, new stuff. Still, maybe it wouldn't be
around for very long. All kinds of disasters
could happen to babies, seeing how
small they were. With any luck,
it would be abducted by aliens,
or eaten by a giant snake. Ben liked
reptiles, he had a book about them
and he looked at it almost
every day. Mum and Dad
used to say "Aren't they
scary, those creatures?" but
Ben didn't think so. *It's a pity
there aren't any buggies with snakes
on them,* he thought.

"And what shall we get for you
then, Ben?" Mum asked. "How about
some new trainers?"

Ben's face changed from cross to excited in an instant. "Can I have the silver ones we saw the other day?" he replied, although he thought he was probably pushing his luck.

"They were a bit expensive." Mum thought about it for a moment and then finally she said, "OK, we'll splash out. If we get the baby the plain orange buggy without the teddies, we'll have enough left over for those trainers."

Ben smiled in surprise. Maybe his mum and dad wouldn't completely forget about him once the baby came.

He began to feel a bit guilty for hoping
the baby would get kidnapped or eaten by
a snake.

The guilt soon wore off though and over
the next few days Ben started worrying all
over again. Sometimes he thought he could
see the new baby sneaking
out of Mummy's
tummy and bouncing
its way through the
clouds. It seemed
as if it was glaring
down at him from the
sky and making him even
more naughty than usual. Ben was sure the
new baby was tricking him into getting his
sums wrong and his spelling was growing
worse all the time. Ben became certain that
the new baby could do some kind of tragic
magic and that nothing good (apart from the
new trainers) would ever happen again.

* * *

One day, Ben went to Ollie and Maxine's house after school. They had just started playing Ollie's new video game in the front room when there was a knock at the door. Ben's dad burst in and said, "We're going to the hospital, Ben, your mum's had the baby."

It had finally happened. Ben didn't want to go. He didn't want to see the new Tragic Magic baby. He wanted to be left alone. "No," he answered firmly.

"What's the matter?" asked his dad. "You haven't wanted to talk about the baby at all for ages now, have you?"

"I'm scared," said Ben, snuggling up to his father and leaning his head against his chest. It felt safer now Dad was beside him.

"What are you scared of?"

"I don't like the new baby and he'll never like me. He's got horrible green hair and yellow eyes and he does Tragic Magic and

makes me feel cross all the time and then I
do things wrong."

"The baby is a she and she looks just like
you. She's got curly dark hair and big brown
eyes and golden skin. She doesn't know
any magic, I promise. And if she did, I'd get
her to sort out a sports car and a win on
the lottery."

Ben nestled
further into his
dad's chest. "It's
not really a girl,
is it?"

"It certainly
is. What do you
think we should
call her?"

27

Ben thought for a while. He hadn't considered that the baby might be a girl. Maybe a girl wouldn't be so bad. He was beginning to feel guilty about the bad thoughts he had had about the baby. He knew that his mum liked flowers, so he said, "How about Daffodil?"

"Not sure about that," replied Dad. "Any other ideas?"

"Rose, then."

"Rose. Hm. That's not bad at all. Let's go and tell Mum and see what she says."

Ben could hardly speak all the way to the hospital. He wanted to see the new baby but at the same time, he didn't. *What if she is as terrible as I've imagined she'll be?* he thought. *What if I have to live with a horrible baby for two whole years?*

They walked down a very long hospital corridor. Ben held his dad's hand tight and hoped nobody would notice.

They reached the ward and Ben could see
Mum as soon as he opened the door. She
was sitting in a chair, holding the new baby.
He crept up to her slowly, wondering what
he might see. His mother pulled back the
blue blanket that was hiding the baby's
face. Ben covered his
eyes for a moment.
Then he dared
himself to look.

The baby did have golden skin, the same as Ben's, but she was tiny and although her mouth was very big she didn't have any teeth, just gums. Her eyes weren't yellow at all, they were brown like Dad had said. She wasn't glaring at Ben – in fact, Ben thought she was almost smiling. She looked quite cute really, like Wilf, when he was a puppy. It was a pity she didn't have fur though. That would have improved her a lot.

"Hello Rose," said Ben and he sat on Mum's bed close by. The baby wasn't that scary at all, not really.

Ben imagined her with fur that began growing on her legs and tummy and arms and face. As it covered her, she looked really beautiful – all soft and cuddly, like Wilf. Ben decided he would get Mum and Dad to buy Rose a nice fur coat.

Stripes

As usual, when Ben woke up, he could hear
Rosie roaring away in her bedroom next
door. She was like an alarm clock. Every
few hours it was the same: she'd scream
and cry, scream and cry. If she hadn't
looked so much like Wilf, Ben would have

got his mum and dad to return her to the supermarket. They'd taken back a radio that hadn't worked properly just the other day, no problem. They'd even got their money back.

Ben got out of bed and went to put on his blue school sweatshirt with the thin red stripes on the waistband, collar and cuffs. It was then that he realized something terrible. He'd become allergic to everything

 stripey – it must have happened overnight.

He knew all about allergies. There had been a programme about them on TV just the other week, and there was this boy who only had to be

near a cat and he got really ill. But people could be allergic to anything, anything at all: washing powder, nuts, chocolate. "Mum!" he shouted in shock, dropping his sweatshirt.

His mother came running in from Rosie's room. "What on earth's the matter?" she said.

Ben pointed to the sweatshirt. "I can't wear it any more. I'm allergic."

"Don't be silly, Ben," his mother replied, picking it up and trying to hand it to him.

Ben wouldn't take it. "I am allergic. I'm allergic to stripes. Look. My eyes are all watery. And I'm wheezy. I don't feel well at all."

His mother looked up to the ceiling and sighed. Then she put on her calm and patient face. "Just get ready, Ben, there's a love. You'll be late otherwise and you'll make Dad late too."

"But I'm allergic—"

"*Ben!*"

"It's not fair, you never believe me," Ben sulked. He started to put his trousers on. Luckily, they were plain, not a single stripe anywhere in sight.

"Go and get washed first," his mother snapped. She wasn't looking calm and patient any more.

Ben went to the bathroom but stopped by the door. He was remembering something terrible. "The bathroom's stripey," he said.

His mother gave him a gentle push and shut the door after him. Then she went to fix a bottle for Rosie.

Ben could hardly move. The blue and
white striped bathroom tiles that lined
the lower half of the walls seemed to be
wobbling like jelly. He could tell too that
the blue and red striped toothpaste, which
he usually had no trouble with, was on the
point of flying at him in a very dangerous
manner. He ducked, just in case.

His dad banged on the door. "Hurry up, Ben," he said.

"I don't feel very well," Ben answered in a trembly voice. "I'm allergic to—"

Ben's dad came into the bathroom. "What is all this nonsense?" he said. Then he added in a softer voice, "Don't you want to go to school?"

Ben did want to go to school. It was painting in the morning and football in the afternoon. But he felt very peculiar, and all the stripes around him seemed to be swirling towards him in a very nasty way. "I am allergic, Dad," Ben said. And just to prove it, he was sick all over his father's shoes.

Ben had to stay in bed for several days. Ollie and Maxine weren't allowed to visit just in case it was catching. Ben thought his mum and dad were being ridiculous. You couldn't catch allergies, everyone knew that. They just came for no reason and made you ill. Ben wouldn't go into the upstairs bathroom. He used the toilet under the stairs, which was painted in plain pale green. And he wouldn't touch anything striped, not even the humbugs his mother bought for him once he was getting better.

* * *

"Your temperature's down, Ben," his dad said as he looked at the thermometer. They were sitting in the living room. Ben was wrapped in a blanket. The television was on. It was football. City were winning 2–0 but their stripey strip was putting Ben off, so most of the time he could hardly bear to watch. "School tomorrow," his dad added.

Ben didn't mind. He would be able to see his friends again and play football. And he wanted to be better again by his birthday in two days' time.

But the next day, when he went to put on his school sweatshirt, he found that its stripes were making him ill again. He started to sweat. He started to wheeze. He could feel his heart beating faster.

"Wear your plain orange one then," his mother said. "I'll tell Miss Lucas why you're not in your uniform."

* * *

Ollie came up to Ben in the playground. "How come you're wearing the wrong sweatshirt?" he said.

"I'm allergic," answered Ben.

"Oh," Ollie replied.

Maxine came over.

"Ben's allergic. He's got to wear orange," Ollie told her.

"I like your proper sweatshirt better," signed Maxine.

"I do too," chipped in Ollie. "You should have been allergic to orange, not blue with red stripes."

"You don't get to choose your allergies," Ben said haughtily.

"I think I'm allergic to Miss Lucas. I came out in a rash yesterday when she told me off about my sums," grinned Ollie.

Ben put his tongue out at him.

"Your tongue's turning stripey," signed Maxine.

Ben ran towards the toilets, desperate to find a mirror. Then he stopped. He'd fallen for it. He could hear his friends giggling behind him.

Ben hadn't realized how many stripes there were in the world until now. It made him feel sick to look at the rest of the class in their uniforms. Tony Evans, who sat at the same table as Ben and was the meanest boy in the class, kept thrusting his blue and green striped pencil case up at Ben's face, laughing himself stupid.

The weather had been grey for ages, but later that morning the sun came out. Planes flew overhead and left long white trails in the clear blue sky. Ben said he wasn't feeling well and was allowed to stay indoors during breaktime.

They did painting afterwards. They were told to choose an insect to draw. Ben wanted to do a big fat bee but he remembered he couldn't. He ended up doing a picture of a spider like the one Maxine was drawing.

"You're copying me," she complained.

"No I'm not. I was going to do a bee."

"Then why didn't you?"

"Stripes," mouthed Ollie.

Maxine didn't look convinced. It sounded like a big fat excuse to her, this allergy to stripes. It seemed to be allowing Ben to get away with everything.

"How was school?" Ben's dad enquired when he came to collect him.

"OK," said Ben, though he wasn't really listening. He was noticing that Tony Evans's mum was wearing a grey and white striped skirt. That whole family was obsessed with stripes, he decided.

"How's the allergy?" asked Dad, as they got into the car.

"Still there," sighed Ben. "There are far too many stripes around, you know."

"I know," his dad replied. He turned on the radio. It was then that Ben noticed the thin green stripes on the cuff of his father's shirt.

Two days later, Ben woke up excitedly on his birthday. He couldn't wait to open his

presents. There
was a new City
kit from his gran.
She was like a mind-
reader, she always
got him the best stuff.
The year before, she'd sent
him swimming things: new swim shorts,
goggles and a diving watch. He loved
swimming, and was the best in his class so
he'd used her presents every single week.

There was a book from Mum and a DVD
about snakes from Dad, which he loved,
but he had been hoping for something
a bit more special. *It's all because
of Rosie*, he thought. Babies
meant there was no money
for anything except nappies and
Babygros. He'd forgotten all about the
silver trainers his mum had bought him
when they'd got the buggy.

* * *

After he had done his homework, Ben went round to Max and Ollie's house. At least he could use their upstairs bathroom, he thought. It was plain white.

"Happy Birthday," said Ollie as soon as Ben arrived. They went up to Maxine's bedroom.

"Mum wanted us to save your present for your party on Saturday, but we thought you'd rather have it now," said Maxine, giving him a large green package.

Ben started to say, "I don't want a birthday party," but he was worried that his friends wouldn't understand. Instead, he concentrated on unwrapping his present. It was a City football and a set of pens with *City* written on the side of each. Ben was speechless with pleasure.

"We knew you'd like them," said Ollie, and they began to talk about the match that City had won 2–0 the other evening. The twins signed their enthusiasm for the game. Ben joined in for a while but he couldn't keep up. "Why don't we talk with words now?" he asked.

This got a sarcastic response with words from Maxine. "Oh dear, he can't keep up. What a shame. Isn't it lucky that I never mind when I can't keep up with you when you're speaking really fast and forget to look at me."

47

Ben felt a little ashamed of himself so he went to sit in the chair by the window, carefully removing a striped cushion with his eyes closed. He hoped he wouldn't be sick. Maxine wouldn't be impressed if he started barfing in her bedroom, and he didn't want any more teasing.

Maxine and Ollie finally finished their conversation so Ben said, "What are you doing on Monday at half term?" His dad was going to be away at a work thing, and he was sure his mother would want to stay indoors with Rosie. If he could say he was doing something with his friends, he might be able to get out of the house. What with Rosie's howling and the bathroom stripes, he thought he could do with being outdoors.

"Mum's taking us out on our bikes," said Maxine.

Ben was disappointed. He wished he hadn't grown out of his bike or he could go too. "Can't you do something else?" he said.

"No," said Maxine firmly, "she's been promising for ages."

"We can see you the rest of the week," said Ollie.

"That's no good. Dad will be back by then."

The twins looked at each other as if they thought Ben was being a pain. Maxine signed something very quickly and Ollie signed back.

"What did you just say?"

"Nothing," said Maxine and Ollie together.

Ben could feel himself getting cross. He hated it when the twins had secrets. It wasn't fair.

"I'm going home now," he said.

"Bye," said Maxine.

"Bye," said Ollie.

They didn't even seem to notice that he was going home because he was too cross to talk to them any more. They didn't even care.

"Is that you, Ben?" called his dad as he came through the front door.

"Yes," Ben called back.

His dad came out of the living room. "Mum and Rosie are in the garden," he said.

Ben followed him outside. It was a bit cold for sitting, and he folded his arms across his chest to keep warm. Mum and Rosie were on a blanket on the grass. They were well wrapped up. Ben couldn't help noticing how cute Rosie was looking in a furry brown jacket with a hood. Wilf was sitting beside her, on his best behaviour. When he played with Ben, he barked and jumped about, but he was always quiet with Rosie because she was so little.

"We've got
a surprise," said
Dad.

Ben really
hoped it wasn't
another baby.
He quite liked
Rosie now, but
one was definitely
enough.

Dad went to the
shed. He took something
out. "What do you think of this?" he said,
holding it up triumphantly.

52

Ben just stared. He could hardly believe it. His dad was holding a brand new bike.

"It's from Rosie," Mum said. "She wanted you to have a special birthday present because you've been such a lovely big brother."

Ben beamed. Good old Rosie. He would never be cross about her ever again. And then he noticed something terrible. The bike was covered in red and black stripes. They were round the handle bars. They were round the mudguards. They were round the whole frame of the bicycle.

Ben tried not to look at it but he couldn't stop. It was so beautiful. He waited for the sick feeling to come. But nothing happened. He waited and waited but it seemed that he had stopped being allergic to stripes.

"I'm cured!" he shouted.

"Yes," said his mother, "we thought you might be."

Ben took the bike from his dad and got
on it. He rode three times
round the garden.

"The twins are going out for a ride at the start of half term. You'll be able to go with them now," his dad said.

Ben remembered Maxine and Ollie's signed conversation, the one he hadn't understood, the secret one. They must have known all along that he'd be going with them.

"Ollie! Maxine!" he called as he rode out of the garden. He couldn't wait to show them his brand new stripey bike.

The Birthday Party

Ben was making cookies in the kitchen with his mother. Rosie was gurgling in her rocker. Wilf was sniffing about in case any cookie dough dropped on the floor beside him.

Ben was good at cooking. He was practically a master chef. "I thought we could make the cake for your birthday party together on Friday," said Mum.

Ben nodded. The thought of making a big fancy cake was so good that for a while it took his mind off his birthday party. He'd been worrying about it for days now but he hadn't told anyone in case they thought he was being silly.

After he put the biscuits in the oven, Ben said, "Can I text the twins to come round now?"

"Yes," replied his mother. "My mobile's in the living room, on the arm of the sofa."

Ben found it and texted: *Can u cum rownd now I am bord.*

Maxine was allowed to have her own mobile phone because it was easier for her to text people than to speak to them. She kept it in her pocket, on vibrate, all the time. Within moments she arrived at the back door but Ollie wasn't with her. He had choir practice after school on Tuesdays.

They went upstairs to Ben's bedroom.

"Are you looking forward to your birthday party?" asked Maxine, sitting on Ben's bed.

"Not really," Ben muttered.

Maxine reached for Ben's arm and turned him towards her so that she could see his lips. Although she often got cross when people forgot to face her when they spoke, all she said was, "What did you say?"

"I don't really want a party."

"Why not?" Maxine signed to him.

Ben used a mixture of speaking and signing to say that he didn't like them.

"Why not?" pushed Maxine.

Ben nearly said birthdays were too noisy but he didn't think Maxine would understand, so instead he answered, "Too many people."

He waited for her to laugh at him, but she didn't. "I know," she replied, "and everybody looking at you as well."

"Do you remember Tony's party?" asked Ben. "Dad said I had to go because his mum looks after Wilf when we go on holiday. Tony kicked me. And he made me eat chocolate stuck on top of a piece of cheese. And last time his mum brought him round, he took two of my cars without even asking. And then he said he hadn't. He didn't even say sorry when his mum found them and made him give them back. It's not fair that he's coming. I wish his mum and my mum would stop being friends. Then we'd never ever have to see each other ever again."

Ben remembered the biscuits he'd made. He and Maxine ran downstairs to switch off the oven before they burned. Then they took two each, placing them carefully on a plate to cool, and went back to Ben's bedroom. "These smell good," signed Maxine. "Are you going to make some for your party?"

"I'm making a chocolate birthday cake," said Ben. Maxine looked impressed.

Ben heard the baby shrieking.

It went on and on and began to get on his nerves, a phrase his mother sometimes used. He wondered what nerves looked like. He thought they must be charcoal grey and wobbly. If only Rosie had some teeth to chew with he would make a biscuit twice her size and shove it in her mouth. It might be just about big enough to keep her quiet for a while.

"If you make your own birthday cake, maybe you'll like your birthday party when it comes," signed Maxine.

"And maybe I won't," Ben replied crossly.

The dreaded day came far too quickly. Ben woke up early. He stayed in bed for a while, staring into the darkness. He had a fluttery feeling in his stomach. *If only I'd been brave enough to tell Mum I didn't want a party*, he thought. Too late now.

He got out of bed slowly and saw his teddy bear tangled up in the bedclothes. He couldn't let Tony see that he slept with a bear when he came to the party. He took him and hid him in his wardrobe. "Sorry, Ted," he said, "but I'm dead if Tony finds you."

Ben went downstairs to the kitchen where his dad was cooking breakfast. He was making Ben's favourite: soft boiled egg with soldiers followed by toast thickly spread with Nutella. It was a special pre-party treat.

Mum came in with Rosie and said to Dad, "Have you seen the cake Ben made last night? It's fantastic."

Dad had been working late the day before so he'd missed the preparation for the party. As his mother put the cake on the table Ben tried to look modest, and failed.

"That is a work of art," said Dad. "Did you do the icing too?"

"Mum helped."

"I bet you can't wait for three o'clock. When I was a boy, I got so excited I couldn't sleep for days beforehand whenever I had a party."

"He isn't the same as you," said Mum, and Ben gave her a grateful look. "Don't get worried about it, will you Ben?" she added. "We've got a surprise for you. We're going to do something you'll really like."

"What?" asked Ben, trying to imagine what it might be.

"Wait and see," said Dad.

"Nothing scary, I promise," Mum told him.

"Can I wear the new football strip Gran gave me?" asked Ben.

"Of course you can," said Dad. "I'll wear my strip as well. We can pretend we're identical twins."

Ben really hoped his dad was joking.

Ben looked in the mirror once he'd put on his new kit. He felt good in it, almost like a different person, nearly as brave as a top-class footballer. He went into the garden and kicked his football about. The new kit seemed to have improved his footy skills. He scored a couple of brilliant goals, kicking the ball straight through the little gap between two trees.

He felt so pleased that he even forgot to be nervous about the party.

"Ben!" his mother called just after three o'clock. "Max and Ollie are here."

Ben had never been shy with Ollie and Maxine before but the party was making him so nervous that as soon as he saw them he got all giggly and dived under the garden table. Luckily, Maxine and Ollie didn't seem to think he was being silly. They dived down under there too and started rolling on the grass. They ended up laughing so much that there were tears in their eyes.

"All right you lot, that's enough, you'll ruin your clothes," said Ben's mother.

They stopped rolling just as the doorbell rang again.

Ben wanted to hide, especially when he saw that it was Tony. But he was friendly enough and gave Ben a big box of chocolates. This was quite nice of him considering he and Ben didn't even like each other.

The other four children
who came to the party – Dan, Tom, Emmie
and Louis – each brought presents with
them too. Ben felt shy again as he looked at
all the birthday gifts, but his Dad said that
he could save opening the presents until
later. This was great because although he
liked presents, Ben didn't like having to
open them in front of everyone, with all
eyes staring.

Just when he was starting to think that
his party might be OK after all, one of the

birthday balloons that were hanging in the living room came loose. It floated through the French windows and into the garden. Tony grabbed it with a shout. He scraped it slowly with his finger nail. Ben shuddered.

"Don't you like this then?" said Tony. He scraped the balloon again and then jabbed it hard. It burst with such a loud bang that Ben jumped. He jumped so high and his heart was beating so fast that he started to shake.

"Who's a baby, who's a scaredy baby?" sang Tony. He ran into the living room and came back with another one. He dangled it in front of Ben, just above his head.

Ben wanted to hide. His good feelings about his party had all disappeared. He felt silly again and not brave at all.

"Leave him alone," said Maxine, prodding Tony with her finger.

"Leave him alone," mimicked Tony in Maxine's flat voice.

For a moment, Ben thought Ollie was going to punch Tony and then the party would be over before it had even started. He almost willed it to happen. But then his dad came into the garden and everyone went quiet. "What's going on?" he asked.

Ben opened his mouth to speak, but Maxine caught his eye and shook her head. He knew she was saying she could fight her own battles.

"Nothing's going on," said Ben, though he was still shaking.

His dad looked as though he didn't believe him but all he said was, "Everyone's here now. It's time to go."

"Go where?" asked Ben.

"It's a surprise," said his mother as she

came into the garden carrying Rosie.

"Are we going in the car?" asked Ben.

"No, we're walking," replied Mum.

"We know where we're going," chorused the twins.

"Tell me," pleaded Ben.

"It's a surprise," said everyone together.

They walked down the road, and then turned left on to the high street.

Ben could hear Maxine telling Tony that he was a great big stupid idiot. She was also reminding him that he had pooed in his pants on their first day in Reception Class.

Tony wasn't saying anything. It was best not to when Maxine was having a go. Ben couldn't think why Tony had picked on her in the first place. It was asking for trouble.

They crossed the road at the traffic lights

and Ben suddenly knew where they were heading. *"Swimming,"* he said.

Everybody laughed and Ben felt shy again.

"You're quite right, Ben, we're having your party at the swimming pool," Dad told him.

"I haven't brought my swimming kit." Ben sounded worried.

"I've got it here," smiled Dad.

"We've all got our swimming things," added Maxine.

Ben began to laugh. He loved swimming. He was the quickest swimmer in his class. And the pool on the high street had big slides that you could go down and you could play ball in the water as well. A party at the swimming pool wouldn't be scary at all.

Ben got into his swimming shorts as quickly as he could. He jumped into the pool.

Maxine jumped in after him. Soon everyone
was in the pool. Everyone except Tony.
He just stood at the edge, not even getting
his feet wet. After a few minutes, Ben got
out of the water and stood beside him.
"Why aren't you getting in? Don't you like
swimming?" he asked.

"Not much," said Tony, trying to make his
voice sound strong.

Ben stared at him. He noticed
that Tony was shivering.

"Are you scared?" asked
Ben in surprise.

"NO!" said Tony, very loudly. But Ben could tell that Tony was. He was absolutely terrified.

Ben couldn't believe it. Under his breath he muttered, *Who's a baby? Who's a scaredy baby?* but he didn't say it out loud. Instead he replied scornfully, "Of course you're scared, it's obvious. Just sit here if you don't want to go in."

"Are you going to tell the others?" muttered Tony.

"I won't tell them as long as you never kick me or call me names again," said Ben, and then he jumped back into the water, giving Tony a big splash as he went.

Ben went down the slide at least twenty-three times and he didn't even go red when the lifeguards sang Happy Birthday.

He just laughed and felt important. And he remembered that when they went home, they would have the chocolate cake he'd made with Mum, and it would have eight candles on it. He hurried up the steps to the diving board. "Mum, Dad, watch this," he shouted. And he dived into the pool the way his dad had taught him. As he landed in the water, he knew that he had just done his best dive *ever*. When he came up to the surface again, everybody clapped. And to his surprise, Tony gave him a big thumbs-up.

The Snake

Ben was watching TV
alone in the living room
one Saturday morning.
His mother had gone
shopping. His dad was in
the kitchen with Rosie.
There was a sharp
knock on the front door.
Ben ran into the hall
but his dad managed to
get there first even though
he had Rosie in his arms.
He opened the door.

"Hello, Mr Croft." It was Mr Norris from next door. He was sounding worried. "I'm sorry to trouble you but I've got a problem," he said. "I was cleaning Charlie's tank this morning and he just slid off. I can't find him anywhere. I think he could have slipped through a crack somewhere or down a drain. I'm afraid he might even have come to your house."

"Who's Charlie?" asked Ben's dad.

"He's one of my pet snakes," Mr Norris replied.

"A *snake*?"

Ben could hear the fear in his dad's voice.

"Don't worry Mr C," said Mr Norris, "he's a big softie really."

Ben imagined what a softie snake might look like. He pictured Charlie with a pink straw hat on his head. It was tied round his long neck with a huge pink and white spotted ribbon.

There were plastic flowers sticking out of it. They were trailing everywhere.

Mr Norris said, "He's that quick, you know. He just shot off."

Ben imagined Charlie the quick snake. His tail was stuffed into a pair of running shorts. He had bright blue super-fast trainers on his feet. He had a baseball cap perched on his head.

"Go back into the living room, Ben," said Dad.

Ben remained where he was. He wanted to hear more about Charlie.

"Go on," his dad repeated.

Ben left very slowly. He kept the door open so he could still hear his dad and Mr Norris talking.

"Is Charlie dangerous?" asked Ben's dad. He sounded really worried now.

"I wouldn't say *dangerous*," answered Mr Norris in a reassuring voice.

"How big is he?"

Ben couldn't hear Mr Norris answer. He pictured their neighbour holding out his hands as far apart as they could go to show Dad how big Charlie was.

His dad said, "As big as *that*? You'll have to call the police."

Ben imagined six policemen all trying to
capture Charlie, whose head was poking
through the window on one side of the
house and whose tail end was poking
through the window opposite. They were
trying to handcuff him but they couldn't
find his arms.

"There's no need for the police," said Mr
Norris. "Charlie will turn up, I'm sure. I just
thought I'd better let you know in case you
saw him and got a fright."

"I've got a fright now," Ben's dad replied
through clenched teeth.

Ben heard the front door close. He ran out into the hall again. "Mr Norris has got a snake! I can't believe it!" He could hardly get the words out. He'd been wanting to see one ever since he'd been given the book and DVD about snakes for his birthday. And now, out of the blue, the opportunity had come.

"I can't believe it either," said Ben's dad. "Mr Norris always seemed like such a nice, ordinary person."

"I wonder how long it will be before Charlie gets back to Mr Norris's house," Ben wondered.

"Not long, I hope." His dad held Rosie so tightly that she yelped. "You mustn't be scared Ben," he added. "I'm sure it will all be OK,

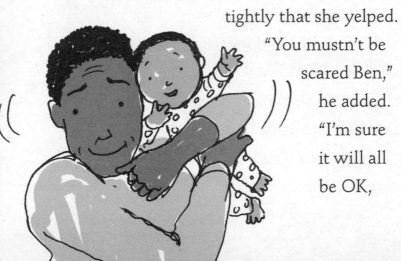

and Mr Norris did say that the snake wasn't dangerous."

Ben felt cross. Why did everybody expect him to be scared all the time? He wasn't at all scared about Charlie, he was very, very excited. A snake was coming round to his house! Things couldn't be better.

"Can I go and see Maxine and Ollie?"

"Yes," said Ben's dad. "And you stay there with them, OK? It will be safer. Off you go!"

Ben ran through the front gate but he had no intention of staying with Maxine and Ollie. He was going to bring them back to his house straight away.

He knocked at the twins' front door. Their mum let him in. "Hello Ben, how are you?"

"Fine thanks. Are the twins home?"

"Maxine's gone to the library with her dad but Ollie's about, he's in his bedroom. Go on up."

Ben ran upstairs and burst into the room. "There's a snake at our house!" he announced.

"A snake?" said Ollie. He turned pale. He stopped putting on his left sock and stood very still. "A *snake*?" he repeated.

"I thought you'd want to see it. It's such a shame that Maxine's out. She'll be so disappointed to have missed it."

Ollie wasn't so sure of that. "Aren't you worried?" he asked.

"Why would I be worried?" replied Ben in surprise.

Ollie had thought that if anyone was going to run a mile from a snake it was Ben. And here he was with a big smile on his face. He was being as brave as twenty-five lions.

"Come on," said Ben, pulling Ollie off the bed. "If you don't hurry up, we'll miss it."

"I want to miss it," Ollie stated.

Ben stared in disappointment
and said, "You don't mean that."

"I mean every word of it," insisted
Ollie.

"You're not scared are you?"

"Of course I'm scared!" Ollie shouted,
in an attempt to get the point across.

Ben didn't get it. "You're scared of
a snake?"

"Flippin' terrified," said Ollie.

"But snakes are beautiful." Ben imagined Charlie at a beauty contest, being awarded first prize. He was slithering along a catwalk (or was that a snake walk?) in a swim suit. People were taking his photograph. The flashing lights were so bright that Charlie had to put some shades on.

"I'm staying here." Ollie was determined.

"Oh please come," pleaded Ben. "I'll give you my second-best car if you come – the black one." It hurt Ben even to think of parting with his model black sports car with the gold lettering and the leopard print upholstery, but some things just had to be done. He waited for Ollie's response but it was slow to come. Ben started to feel impatient. It was the deal of a lifetime, what was there to think about?

"OK," Ollie said at last. He'd been envious of that car for ages. It was just a pity he had to go snake hunting in order to get his hands on it.

"Just going back to Ben's house!" Ollie called out to his mum as they left. He was careful not to mention snakes.

In Ben's living room, Dad was still holding Rosie, chewing the fingers of his free hand and bending down every now and then with extreme caution to see if any snakes were lurking. "What are you doing back here?" he asked.

"We thought we'd play in my room," answered Ben. Then he added, "Ollie's mum is very busy. She didn't want us cluttering up the house."

This was a fib, so Ollie looked shocked. He didn't say anything though. He was thinking about the black sports car.

Ben's dad
put Rosie in her
playpen. He went
to the cupboard under
the stairs. He got out a
cricket bat and a net. He also grabbed a big
ball of string, some scissors and a pen knife.

"What are *they* for?" asked Ben.

"That snake won't give us any trouble,
I promise," replied Ben's dad with such
desperate firmness that Ben started to
giggle.

His dad gave him a concerned look. What
was so funny about such an awful situation?
Had hysteria started to set in? "Are you
OK?" he asked.

"Of course I am, Dad, I'm not a bit scared," replied Ben.

"I am," said Ollie, but he was determined to stick it out. That car was almost in his reach.

"Go upstairs then, both of you. And if you see a sign of anything out of the ordinary, you must call me straight away."

Ben ran upstairs and Ollie trailed behind him.

"What if it's in your bedroom?" asked Ollie.

"Wouldn't that be brilliant?" said Ben.

"You go in first." Ollie tried to control his voice, but it came out as a squeak.

There was no sign of a snake in Ben's bedroom. *So disappointing*, he thought. "Where would you hide if you were a snake?" he asked Ollie.

"Under the bed," answered Ollie, trembling.

"Ben looked under the bed. "No, he's not here. Never mind."

"He might be in the wardrobe," suggested Ollie. He hid behind Ben's toy box just in case.

Ben opened the wardrobe door. "No, he's not here. Perhaps he got into the toy box."

Ollie jumped and ran to the other side of the room. Ben lifted the lid of the toy box. "No, not here. Where else could he be?"

"He might not be in your room at all," Ollie pointed out. "He might be in the hall or in Rosie's room."

"No, he's definitely here somewhere, I know about snakes. "It's just a question of finding him," said Ben stubbornly.

Ben imagined Charlie as a master of disguise, hiding from everyone. Sometimes he was dressed like a boy. Sometimes he was dressed like a girl. Sometimes he made himself look like a door. Sometimes

he looked like a chair. He was so good at
disguising himself that no one could ever
see him, even though he was right under
their noses all the time.

"I know," said Ben. He went to the corner
of the room where there was a little built-
in cupboard. "He's in there, I just know he
is." Ben opened the door. And a big brown
snake with a zig-zag pattern all over
it slithered out.
Ollie screamed.
Ben's dad came
running up the
stairs with Wilf the
dog. Wilf took one
look at the situation
and ran back downstairs
again. "Cowardy custard!"
called Dad as Wilf's tail
disappeared.

Ben's dad had the net, the cricket bat, the scissors, the string and the pen knife in his hands. "It's all right, I'm here, don't panic anyone," he shouted.

Ben had never been further from panicking in his whole life. "You don't need all that stuff, Dad. Charlie won't hurt anyone." Ben was holding Charlie in his arms, stroking him and making gentle noises. The snake was looking contented. He was half asleep. If he'd been a cat, he would have been purring.

"I'll take him back to Mr Norris," Ben said. "Come on, Ollie."

Ollie didn't move. He just picked up
Ben's black sports car and held it tightly
to his chest.

Ben went downstairs, carrying Charlie.
He'd expected a snake to feel slimy but he
wasn't at all – in fact, he felt quite rough.
Ben continued to stroke him.

Ben walked past Rosie, who was in her
playpen, her chubby fists beating slowly
on a toy drum. It was the only thing in the
house that made more noise than she did.
As she saw Ben, she stopped and smiled
in approval.

Outside in the street, a crowd of the
neighbours had gathered. They'd heard
there was a snake on the loose. They'd
come to see if it had been captured yet.
As Ben appeared on the doorstep, there
was a gasp from the crowd. There was
Ben, holding the snake, brave as anything.
A big cheer went up. Ben just stood there,

stroking Charlie
and looking rather
pleased with himself.
His mother appeared,
hurrying towards him with
bags of shopping in her hands.
"Ben!" she shouted in fright. "Put
that thing down right now!"
"It's all right," called Ben, "he's really
friendly. He isn't dangerous at all."

He held up the snake.
People started taking photos
with their mobile phones.

Mr Norris came out. "Oh
you've found him," he said.

"Well done, lad. You're a born
snake handler if ever I saw one."

Ben beamed.

Two days later, Ben's picture appeared on
the front page of the local paper. Someone
had sent in one of the photos they'd taken
with their mobile phone. In the picture,
Ben was smiling. The crowd was smiling.
But Charlie the snake was wriggling his
head away from the camera flashes, as
if he were frightened of all the attention.
And the newspaper headline said: BRAVE BEN
SCARES SNAKE!

Jacqueline Roy

My dad was Jamaican and my mum was English.
I was born in London but I moved to Manchester
some years ago to teach English at Manchester
Metropolitan University. I started writing when
I was seven (not very well, I've improved since!) and
I love being able to write for children and adults.
Being Ben came about because I remembered being
scared of lots of things when I was young. My mum
used to tease me and call me Cowardy Custard. She
was very funny about my fears and this helped me
to be braver. Everyone's scared of some things, but
everyone can be brave too, just like Ben.

Margaret Chamberlain

has illustrated many books for all ages; this is her
first about a little boy finding a huge snake...
She lives by the sea in Lyme Regis with her husband,
Ian Dicks, also an illustrator. Margaret likes to walk
along the seafront, but has no ambition to go out
in a boat. "The best thing about the sea is when
the moon shines on it; it's the most beautiful sight.
The other wonderful thing is watching all the funny
dogs that arrive with their owners in the summer."